The Picnic

written by Amy Jo
illustrated by James Williamson

 **McGraw-Hill
School Division**

New York   Farmington

Turkey likes to eat.

Goose likes to eat.

Monkey likes to eat.

Gorilla likes to eat.

Pig likes to eat.

Alligator likes to eat.

Now we need to rest!